This Journal Belongs To:

Princess Elaenor

(the best princess to ever exist)

Hardcover ISBN: 979-8-9887169-6-9
Paperback ISBN: 979-8-9887169-7-6
eBook ISBN: 979-8-9887169-8-3
Cover & Layout by: Maggie Tortoledo Designs

Age 5

Me and mama went to the lake today.
We had soooo much fun!

Nora

(recovered)

Toby pushed me down the hill today.

Mama said he's not a very happy boy.

Why is Toby so sad?

Age 5

Nora

(recovered)

Age 6

Auntie Ami is getting so big! She said the baby is still far away. I hope it's a girl. I want a friend to play with.

Mama says it's a girl. Theo is just as excited, but Toby is mad about it. He said he doesn't want another person in his house, but his house is REALLY BIG.

Nora

(recovered)

Age 6

Theo took pastries from the cook today. We ate them by the lake and they were soooooooo good!

We're hiding from Toby. He's so mean to me.

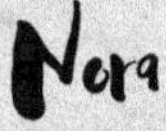

Nora

(recovered)

mama and Father are making me go with them to Rakooja?? I don't know how to spell it.

I don't wanna go, but I will see Emery at least.

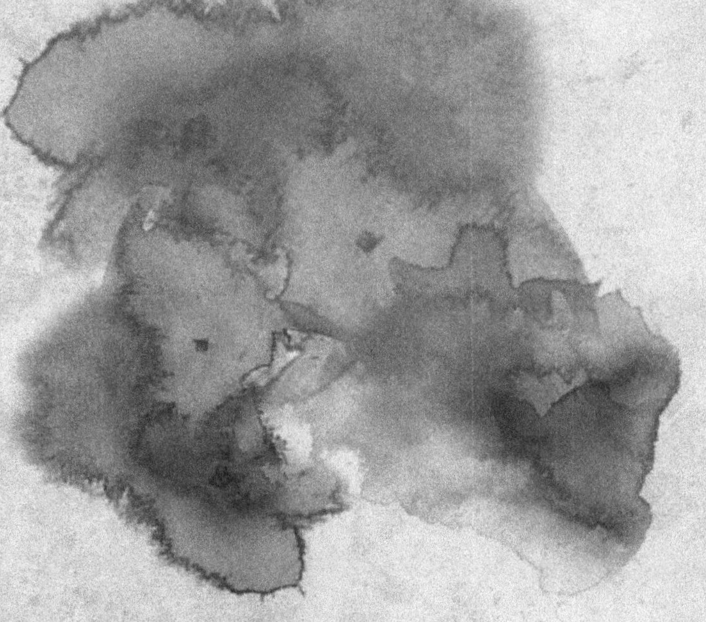

Nora

(recovered)

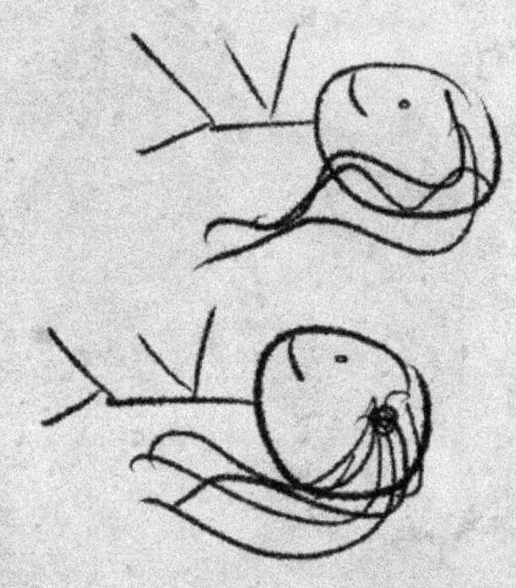

You will not believe what happened! Scarlett didn't believe me. There was a boy at Em's house. He had purple eyes, which is superrrr weird. but he was so mean to me and Em.

Mama said his name was like Ned or something. I dunno. Em and I threw water at him and ran. He deserved it.

Nora

I am finally 7!

Mama is taking me to see Theo and Toby today. I don't wanna see Toby but I have too. Auntie Ami is getting super BIG. And she keeps telling me I'm going to marry Toby one day. I don't wanna marry Toby.

I wanna marry Theo and have pastries every day.

Nora

(recovered)

Toby pushed me down the hill again. We were playing in the trees like always but he just looked so angry. And then when Theo held my hand, Toby pushed me.

When I went to find mama and Auntie Ami, auntie was so mean. Mama said it's because the baby is so close to being born.

Maybe she will come today and we can share a birthday!

Nora

Mama isn't feeling too well. She keeps bleeding and kass has been helping her.
Father refuses to come see her. Why won't he? Isn't he worried about her?

I am worried about her.

Nora

(recovered)

I don't remember anything.

There are pages ripped out of here. Did I do that?

The master said mama is dead.

They won't tell me how.

HOW?

how??

WHY??

The dreams are really bad. I just see lots of fire. What is on fire?

Mender Jax gave me some sweet stuff. It helps me sleep. It scares away the dreams.

N

The sweet stuff isn't working anymore. Not unless I take a lot. But Master Akin said that I can't take that much or I'll end up like mama.

Is that how she died?

Father is mad that I am not happy.

How can I be happy?

My mama is dead and I don't remember anything.

N

Master Akin said I should use this journal to say my feelings. Is that not what I am doing? Father said I had to listen.

Scarlett said they can go to hell.

(i like her answer better)

kassius is gone.
Father says he killed mama.

Is that true?

Why is <u>everyone</u> leaving me??

Father says I must practice my adult writing if I am to be respected some day.

How's THIS father?

i wish you died instead of mama

N

Everything is the same, yet different.

I am so alone.

n

King Evreux visited today. Every year like clockwork.

He looks at me funny, but I must remain respectful, apparently.

But when he comes, Father gets angry.

The new lashing on my back is evidence of that.

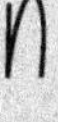

I'm 11 today.

No one noticed. No one even pays attention to me. Scar calls me a secret.

How can I be a secret if I have lived here my whole life?

I have, haven't I?

n

Laenie and Rhea are sick. Some sort of bug going around.

Father won't let them in the palace, but Scar is here. She wants to go home, but Father won't let her.

Can't he just give her some medicine?

Master Akin called it a plague. He said it is a type of sickness that kills people. Rhea and Laenie are okay, but most of their family died.

A lot of funeral pyres and burials happening today.

I miss mama.

n

I bled today.

I thought I was dying, but Estelle said I am okay.

I don't feel okay. I thought I was sick like my mama was before she died.

I feel so alone here.

Nearly a month.

I was asleep for nearly a whole month. My back is sore and the creams the menders use smell too sweet.
I am so tired. How can that be? I have been sleeping so much.

I have more sleeping draft to take. I should take it.

When will I be free of my father?

n

A raven arrived for my father today.

Tobias has turned 18. He is ready to wed.

I'm not.

I'm not.

I'm not.

n

One year.

One more year until I can leave.

Do I want to?

Leaving means marriage...

Staying means my father.

What do I do?

n

My measurements were taken today.

A wedding dress will be made.

n

None of them will look at me. Not Scar, Laenie, or Rhea. They whisper about themselves and then stay quiet when I come near.

I saw Scar being ushered into my father's bed chambers yesterday. She looked scared.

She won't talk to me about it.

What did my father do?

5 months left....

n

The dreams won't stop. They are just getting worse.

I drank all the sleeping draft.

I hope I don't wa

Two months.

Two.

TWO

n

I turn 18 next week. I sent my ladies away so that I could sort through things myself. I even banished Estelle from my room. I regret that already.

Instead of packing, I am writing on a piece of paper as if it some how has the answers I am seeking.

What am I doing?"

I am excited to start a new life, but the rumors about my betrothed make him sound like a monster.

Will I survive Noterra?

9 days

N

Hello again.

I found this journal hidden in the vanity, no doubt one of my new ladies.

Did they read it? So much has happened today, or I guess the past few days.

I awoke today inside the infirmary at Noterra. The palace master, Apollo, said that I had been through something terrible. How would he know?

I was poked and prodded. I was <u>checked</u>. I was told I was impure, as if I didn't already know.

As if I didn't live through it myself.

I am in pain. My limbs burn, my core feels as if it was ripped. I ran so fast and so far, and in the end, it didn't matter. He still caught me.

He still killed Erik.

How am I supposed to move on? How am I supposed to be okay? King Evreux said he spoke to my father. Will he come get me? Am I even more of a disappointment to him?

Don't even get me started on Tobias. He's...everything I always imagined him to be. Kind, caring, strong, powerful. But I also met Theo. He's soft, protective, warm.

Why are they so different?

Why is my life so different?

I feel like I have lost so much in the last few days.

I lost Erik.

I lost my purity.

I lost my sanity.

What happens now?

Elaenor

Tobias took me on a tour of the grounds. It's only been a few hours since my last entry, but I just need to talk to someone, even if it's myself.
Every person here seems to love Tobias. They treat him like a god. That's good right? But at dinner...the way he and his brother look at each other.
They hate each other.
If I had a brother, or any sibling, I couldn't imagine feeling anything but love. And Theo...the way he looks at ME. I feel something, a warmth that starts in my chest and ignites my limbs as if he is setting me on fire. I can't feel that.

He is to be my brother in law.

And even now, from the comfort of my bath, I hate that I feel guilty. As if Tobias almost caught me doing something treasonous. But all we did was look at one another.

That's it. Right?

Elaenor

He kissed me.

He touched me.

And I panicked. I tried to enjoy it. I did, but then this pain started between my legs. Blood was every where. I could barely breathe and Tobias ran. He RAN.
Then it was Theo. Theo took my to the infirmary. Why does that feel as if it happened before? The feel is his arms around me? It feels so familiar.

Tobias asked me not to speak to Theo anymore. to be fair. I can see why. Theo tells me things Tobias doesn't want me to know. That only makes me want to speak to him more.

He also saw my scars.

Today was a busy day. It was too much.

Elaenor

I am safe.

I am not in Chatis.

I am not on fire.

People are not dying.

It is NOT REAL.

Elaenor

The King attacked me today. I can still feel his hands roaming my body and pulling at my skirt. I can feel his hot breath on my neck. I can hear him saying how beautiful my mother was and how HE can give me a child.
A CHILD.

Not his son.

HIM.

I don't think I am safe here.

I don't think I will ever stop seeing the men who keep trying to claim me as their own.

And my memories. I knew my memories were gone. but I grew up here. In this palace. What is going on?

I want to go home. At least Erik is alive. I have Erik.

Elaenor

I met Sybil. The horse sourced for me and named after my mother. Tobias called her a Percheron, some sort of fancy rare breed.

Not only that. I learned my mother may have loved Evreux. And me...

I was attacked the day my mother died. The person who killed her, attacked me. I was missing for weeks. I was presumed dead.

I was the secret princess to be kept safe. My father was trying to protect me.

He was protecting me.

Elaenor

I have never been more terrified in my life.

I felt her wet hair. I felt the fear coursing through my veins. She was REAL.

But Tobias said she wasn't.

I took off last night and ended up in Rakushia. I was attacked - again. These men in cloaks drugged me. They tried to take me. I rode right into their arms because SHE was chasing me.

She was real.

SHE IS REAL.

She was leading me to Rakushia - but why?

I am not crazy.

    I am not insane.

It was real.
It was real.
It was real.

Happy birthday to me.

Elaenor

He touched me.

Twice.

And I enjoyed it. BEGGED for it.

Is it still considered a sin to find pleasure before marriage if my purity is already gone?

Do I even care at this point?

We didn't leave the room all day and I can say, without a doubt, this was the best birthday I ever had.

But I can't shake the feeling that none of this is real. Will I wake up back in the trees with an unknown man on top of me? Or when I fall asleep tonight, will I wake back up in Tobias's arms?

What part of this is real?

Elaenor

The King attacked me. My hand is bleeding. my cheek numb from where he slapped me. He attacked me and fully prepared to rape me.

The KING.

Tobias got there just in time. But he was so frantic. I can still see his eyes. he looked so scared. But I was also scared. He didn't care about me. So why do I feel bad for him.

Here I am. In a red wedding dress. Getting blood wiped off my face and my hair fixed. writing in this stupid journal. feeling bad for a man who attacked me. I shouldn't. I should focus on something else.

Like I am getting married.

Oh god.

I am getting married today.

Elaenor

Barely any time has passed and a different King has hit me.

A different King because Evreux is dead. He died. Moments ago. While Tobias and I stood over him and watched. He's dead. He loved my mother.
What is going on?

And Theo. Theo proclaimed his love and told me that he couldn't stand by and watch me marry his brother. He said I was always supposed to be his, and then he kissed me. Passion. fear. love. All of that was poured into that kiss. Nothing with Tobias ever felt like that.
But I pulled away. Because I am to be wed to his brother any minute.
But what I didn't expect was for Tobias to attack Theo. And then, hit me.

Tobias hit me.

Here I am. For the third time today. Getting cleaned up and readied for a wedding I don't even know is going to happen.

My soon to be husband hit me.
The king is dead.
Theo loves me.

Elaenor

I am married...

I tried a new wine today and nearly drowned in the bath.

But I didn't feel like I was in the bath. I felt like I was in Chatis.

It felt like I was on fire.

Elaenor

Theo left last night. He came to say goodbye to me.

He wanted me to go with him, but I couldn't.

And now I am being stuffed into another gown. A nother layer of creams and paints plastered to my face.

I am to be crowned in a few short moments.

I will be a Queen.

Elaenor

So much has happened.

I am the Queen.

But more importantly, Jeremiah is here. The man who attacked me. The man who almost killed Erik. He's here. He is the Master of Coin and Tobias doesn't believe me.

And then he hit me. Again.

My husband hit me and then tried to rape me. I am so scared.

I have to be strong. I can't let them know I am scared.

What do I do?
What do I do?
What do I do?

Elaenor

I had too much wine. I don't remember falling asleep.

But here I am. Wet hair, a new night dress I have never seen before.

An empty bed. Warm wine on the bedside table.

How long has it been?

Elaenor

I saw him again.

The man I saw in Chatis. The man I have seen in my dreams.

He was HERE.

His green eyes are so bright, almost as if they glow. And his face, sculpted out of stone. I've seen him before, but the familiarity I feel is something else entirely.

He won't tell me who he is or what he wants. He won't tell me anything.

And then I woke up in the bath. Again.

What is going on? Am I going mad?

Is any of this real???

Elaenor

I sent a letter to my father with Erik five days ago and no response or return has come.

I am worried.

Elaenor

It has been ten days since Erik left.

Where is he??

On top of that. I joined the council today. Tobias blamed me for a war that is yet to start. He's blaming me for deaths that haven't happened yet.

But it is HIS fault too.

And then he kissed me. And told me he loved me. And I let him. I let him use me.

Who am I?

Elaenor

I almost died.

AGAIN.

Jeremiah drugged me. He came into my room. He tried to kill me. Even now it hurts to breathe. My neck burns, my throat on fire. He tried to kill me because Tobias didn't believe me.

Only to be saved and then be told that Tobias got another woman pregnant. He has a child yet to be born out there and this woman is at court.

He was with this woman while I was being attacked.

I was alone.

I am alone.

Elaenor

I am married.

I was raped.

I was attacked.

I ran.

But now? Now I feel safe. I feel at home with Tobias. I feel loved.

Right?

Elaenor

Tobias hit me again.

Elaenor

I am a queen.
A queen of an entire country.

The festivities begin tomorrow, but why are my thoughts only of him and not my husband?

I'm lost.

I wish I had my friends.

Elaenor

Scarlett is here.

My best friend is moving to court. Tobias surprised me with her today. she was my wedding gift. and I am actually happy about it.

Scarlett is here.

But she's here WITH Theo.

She's engaged to him as of two seconds ago when I watched Theo propose to her from my balcony.

But I also saw HER. Nylah is her name. The woman pregnant with my husband's child.

She's a proper woman. not a child like me. She's gorgeous. She loves him.

I have more people around me than I ever have and yet I sitll feel so alone.

Theo is here. But he's not mine.

He never was. But. gods. I wish it was me.

Elaenor

He is testing something. I found his journal. Something about dosages and weight.

He's testing some sort of drug. What is he doing?

Elaenor

Erik is dead.

He's dead.

He died in Chatis because I sent him out while he was still recovering.

It's my fault. MINE.

I haven't left bed all day. I don't think I can.

Every time I wake up, something else has happened. Why can't I wake up and be happy?

I just want to be happy.

Elaenor

I saw him again. I got in the bath, closed my eyes, and pictured him.

And he appeared.

I am mad. I have to be. But he told me not to fight if I ever fear for my life. How could he ask that of me? Why wouldn't I fight.

But he also told me his name.

Enzo.

Why does the sound of those letters feel like a homecoming? Feel like an awakening?

Who is he?
Who is he?
WHO IS HE?

Elaenor

I dreamt that Tobias attacked me. That he hit me and strangled me and that I passed out from lack of air.

I dreamt that he tried to kill me.

And I awoke in that spot. but I was perfectly fine. No bruises. No injuries. Just an ache in my head from the alcohol I consumed.

I don't remember much from last night. but what I do remember. I should regret.

But I don't.

Elaenor

She's gone.

Scarlett is gone.

I can hear her laugh as if she's actually there, but when I close my eyes...

he's dead.

they are all dead.

but HE IS DEAD.

DEAD.

THEO IS DEAD

all I see is blood

help me

My country is gone.
My friends are gone.
Theo is gone.

Everything.

All of it.

What is next?
~~What~~ WHO is next??

i only have one goal. one reason to be alive

revenge

Day 3

I think it has been three days. I can't recall.

Time is moving weird.

Days are blurring together. Has it been only days? Has it been weeks?

I have a T branded on my stomach. I don't remember when I got it.

I don't remember a lot of things.

I don't even remember the snow starting to fall. Now it's already Spring. How long has it been?

What is happening?

Elaenor

Day 14

My name is Elaenor Rosenthal.

I am the Queen of Noterra.

I am married to Tobias.

My mother's name was Sybil.

Theo is dead.

Donny is dead.

Scarlett is dead.

Tobias killed them.

TOBIAS.

REMEMBER TOBIAS DID IT!

REMEMBER

Elaenor

This isn't living.

This is surviving.

Day 43??

I am missing time. Between the drugs and the dungeon. I don't know what month it is.

Lydia keeps my journal hidden. She helps me remember.

He can't find. it
He can't find it.
He can't.

he can't find it

Elaenor

My name is Elaenor Rosenthal.
I am the Queen of Noterra.
I am married to Tobias.
My mother's name was Sybil.
Theo is dead.
Tobias killed him.

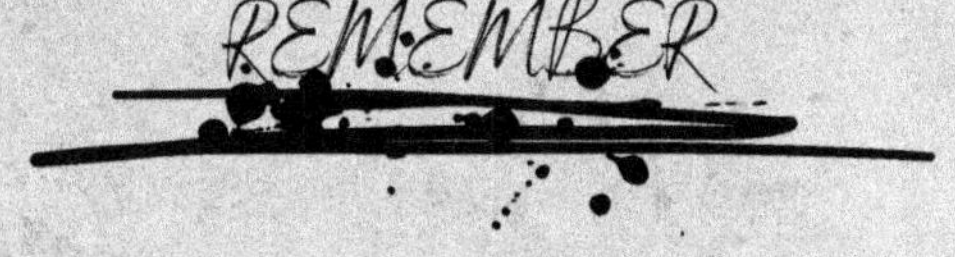

Elaenor

Day 61 (I think)

Davel touched me.
It wasn't the first time. It won't be the last. That is, if my memory is accurate.
I don't know if it is.

I am so tired.
So damn tired.

When will I be free?

why

why me?

WHY

why why why why

Day ??

Here I lay in a warm bath with Lydia's hands massaging my scalp.

But all I see is the blood covering every inch of me. I have been in the dungeon for an indiscernible amount of time. I don't remember what the sun feels like. What food tastes like.

When it gets quiet. I hear my bones snapping.

My tendons ripping.

I can taste the blood in my mouth as I bite back my screams.

He wants to break me.

He can't find out he already has.

Elaenor

Day 72 (i think)

72 scratches on the back of the night stand, but I don't know if that is accurate.

I spoke for the first time in weeks today. But I also saw Thelonious. He's here. He looks ill, and I suppose he is. My heart breaks for him. Emery and Aunt Lyla are gone. Dead. I know what it feels like, but my heart breaks for him all the same.

At court today, I also learned there was an attack on Tellavid, but when that poor woman said the men come from inland and not the sea...all I could think was that we have no enemies here. So who really attacked our harbor?

As if this wasn't already a harrowing day, Tobias asked for Thel's support in being named High King. What would that even mean?

Tobias also touched me today. I hate to admit that I enjoyed it. I enjoyed the feel of him caring about me. Making sure I enjoyed it. What does that say about me?

Elaenor

Day 73

Davel attacked me today. Even worse than he ever has before.

I got away and found Tobias.

He believed me.

He BELIEVED me.

Then he cared for me. He held me as I cried and ensured I was okay.

He seemed like Tobias again. My Tobias. The version of my husband I fell in love with. I can't help but feel hopeful, relieved, at the thought of him returning. At the thought of things maybe getting better.

Will I be okay now?

Elaenor

Day ???

I don't know how long I slept. How many days passed while I lay unconscious.

Tobias sewed the crown to my head. I felt each prick of the needle. I felt each time Apollo pulled the thread through my skin. The pain was indescribable and I finally screamed. But when I closed my eyes, I saw purple. Purple eyes, dark hair, fear on his face.

Who are you?

I also saw Nylah, or maybe just heard her. I don't know if it is real or not, if she truly came to my side.

She begged for my help. She said Tobias was going to take her son. She has a SON. If that was real, if any of this was, Tobias will turn that little babe into a monster. She has to save him. She has to get him and herself out of Noterra.

It's the only way.

Maybe she could find help for me too?

Elaenor

Day 1 with Cyn

She's gone. Nylah is dead.

And her son, Cynfael, has been placed in my arms and declared mine. He is not my son. He is not my child. But he no longer has a mother.

What am I supposed to do? Of course I will care for him. I could never leave him helpless. He looks like her. Red hair, tiny freckles. The only part of Tobias I see is the ocean in his eyes. The ocean that I wanted to believe was home.

Even now, as he sleeps in the bassinet beside me, I feel this overwhelming urge to scream and cry. Nylah. Gods. Poor Nylah. All of this has made me almost forget about the raven I saw. The one who claimed he was Enzo.

But that can't be real. I'm going mad.

An insane woman is being forced to raise a motherless child.

Oh, gods. What do I do?

Elaenor

Day 4 with Cyn

Tobias has barely come to our chambers since he placed Cyn in my arms. He comes in for what he claims is 'his', meaning my body. He says hello to his son, and then he leaves until the next day. I should feel saddened by that thought, but I'm not.

Today is the first day of peace I have had since... I can't remember.

Cyn is talking to himself from where the nursemaid is rocking him with a bottle. He's a fairly happy babe. Apollo has come in to do checks on him quite regularly. While I stay far away from him, he did inform me that Cynfael is three months old.

Three months old and has already had a horrible childhood.

I will protect him. I don't care what it takes.

He will be safe.

Elaenor

Day 11 with Cyn

He was unruly today. He cried and cried and didn't want me.

He wants his mother.

Tobias blamed me and had the nannies and nursemaid take him away. In the hours he was gone. Tobias tortured me. He didn't even take me to the dungeons. He did it right on the marble of our bedroom.

Sliced and sliced until I was laying in a pool of blood that looked identical to the one I stared at months ago....when Theo died.

He hit me. Kicked me. Raped me. Repeat and repeat and repeat.

The entire time. I didn't fight. I didn't cry.

I didn't scream. I have to be strong.

It's not just my life anymore. It's Cyn's too.

Elaenor

Day 28 with Cyn

Nearly a month has passed. I have Malia on the look out for someone - anyone - who can take in Cyn. I don't think I'll be around much longer.

My days are dwindling. I can feel it.

Who will protect him when I am gone?

Elaenor

Book Series

<u>The Diadem</u>
Glass and Bone
Cages and Crowns
Elaenor (can be read at any time)

<u>The Soulless</u>
Persephone

Author Note

This journal started as a passion project and ended up as a way to bridge the gap between book one and two. I wanted more. I wanted tears. I wanted memories. And what better way to provide that by having a journal of those very things?

This journal contains spoilers for Glass and Bone as well as Cages and Crowns. With that being said, it can be read at any time.

Think of it as the AB of the TOG world. Get it? No?

XO Celaena

About the Author

Celaena Cuico (sell-ay-nuh coo-we-co) is a 28 year old bisexual that was born and raised in Southern California. She was raised with two parents and an older sister, as well as an army of pets. Celaena endured hardships such as an abusive significant other and the unknown that comes with moving across the country twice for a job. She is the author of The Diadem, a series about a young girl thrown into a life of jumping from kingdom to kingdom to survive, as well as the author of a new series called The Soulless, which follows servants of Lucifer.

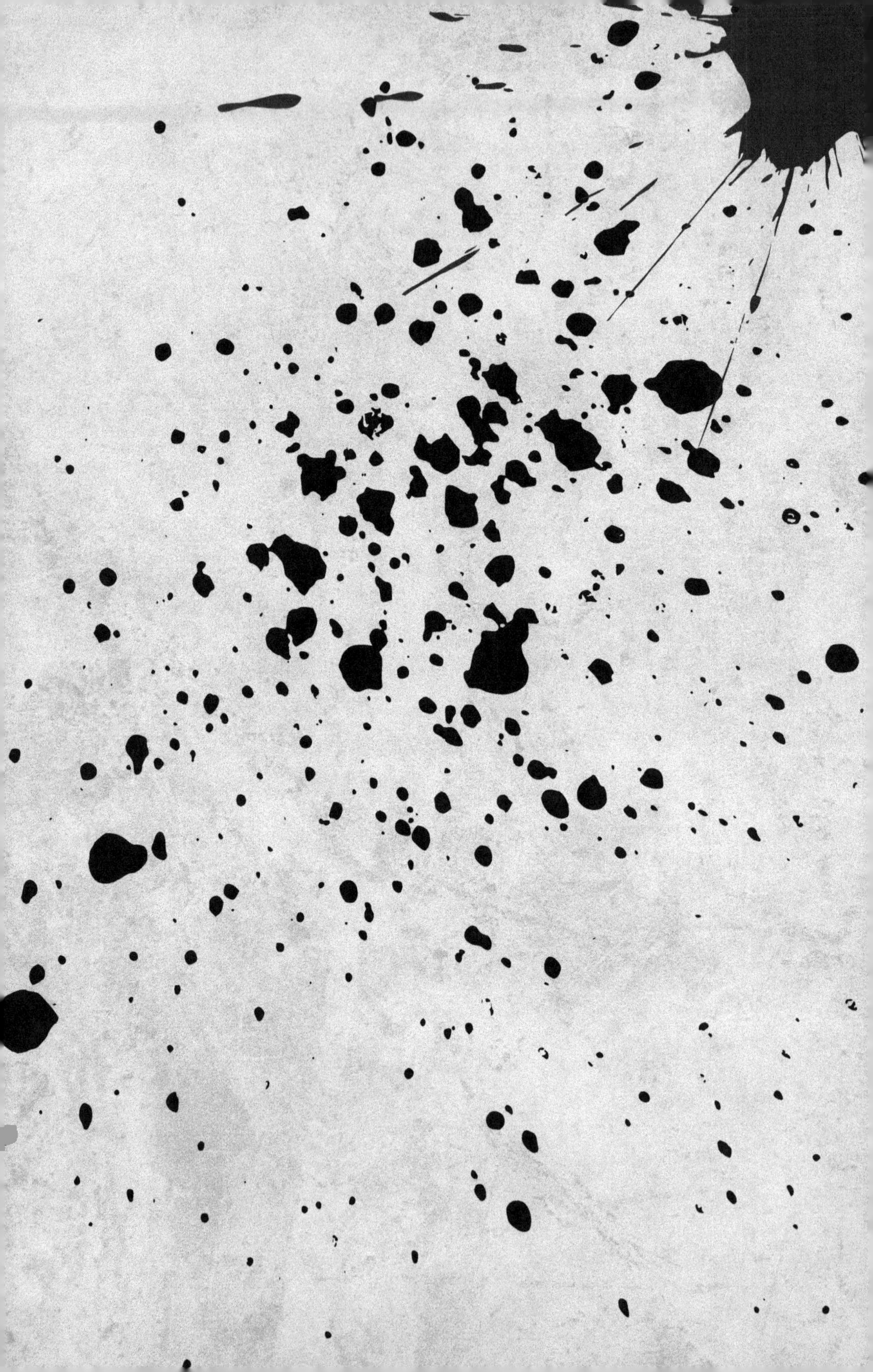